Praise for
JULIAN RODRIGUEZ
EPISODE ONE: TRASH CRISIS ON EARTH

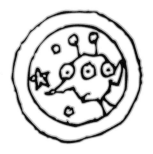

JULIAN RODRIGUEZ

RODRIGUEZ

EPISODE TWO
INVASION OF THE RELATIVES

Dear Mothership,

I regret to inform you that my latest report, *Invasion of the Relatives*, may have been intercepted.

Indeed, lately my home base has been crawling with suspicious life-forms. It is possible that one of them will try to use the report as a means of exposing my Earth research to the planet at large.

But fear not, Mothership — I will do whatever is necessary to contain the info-breach and return the situation to "normal."

As I have said before, these beings are no match for me.

I am, after all,

Julian Rodriguez
Federation Officer, First Rank

JULIAN RODRIGUEZ

EPISODE TWO
INVASION OF THE RELATIVES

Alexander Stadler

SCHOLASTIC PRESS ▪ NEW YORK

UNHYGIENIC!

UNHYGIENIC!

These creatures
are not only barbaric,
they are also UNHYGIENIC!

Mothership:

Please,
First Officer Rodriguez,
slow down.
We understand
that you are in danger,
but we are unable
to comprehend
the nature of
your transmission.

My apologies, Mothership.
I was in crisis mode and had
let my emotions get the best
of me. I am now ready to
begin transmission.

Mothership:

Very well.
Continue.

Mothership, I believe I may have been infected with mini-brain DNA.

Mothership:

*How is this
possible?*

I am afraid it has much to
do with the bizarre behavior
of the common Earthling during
festival time.

Mothership:

Festival time?
We are not sure
we understand.
Can you explain
the events that
led up to
the contamination?

Certainly, Mothership. This
festival they indulge in is
indeed a barbaric affair—not
surprising, given the generally
primitive nature of their
society.

During this particular
festival, the living quarters
are festooned with natural

debris. Groups of genetically
linked mini-brains from
different localities are
invited to come and feast on
hideous local specialties.
   Disguised as I am as a junior
member of their clan, I am
often forced to participate in
the disgusting preparations.

The Parental Units are
at their most unstable and
unpredictable during these
periods. They invariably

whip themselves into a
pointless frenzy in an attempt
to beautify our base.

Mothership:

One question
before you proceed.
Why are you
not relaying this
transmission from
your usual
base of operations?

During these festivals,
The Units remove me from my
personal sleep chamber and
relocate me to a
subterranean
containment facility.

Mothership:

*Is this why
your life-force
readings are so
low, Officer?*

That certainly has much to do with it. On this occasion, The Paternal Unit prepared a suffocating cocoon for me to use as a rest inducer.

I believe the theory is that lack of oxygen will bring on sleep. He even had the audacity to suggest that I might enjoy it.

Mothership:

*The mini-brains
commandeer
your quarters?*

Yes, Mothership. And they separate me from my lieutenant. The Parental Units blame the allergies of the genetically linked minis. But as far as I can see, the only thing they are allergic to is normal behavior.

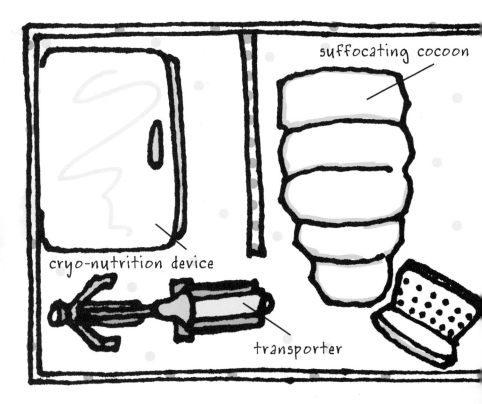

suffocating cocoon

cryo-nutrition device

transporter

Ripley is sequestered in
another part of the belowground
containment facility that
houses the hygieno-swirl and
the cryo-nutrition device.

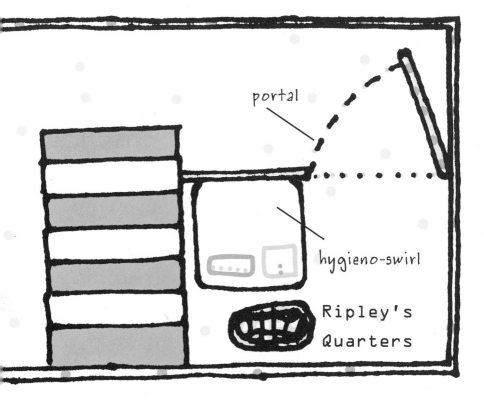

portal

hygieno-swirl

Ripley's
Quarters

Mothership:

*Tragic to be torn
away from
one's fellow
officers.*

True, Mothership. It is possible that The Units separate me from my companion because they believe I am weaker when I am working alone. Perhaps there is some truth in this. But this is no time for sentiment.

Mothership:

*True, time is
of the essence.
Proceed.*

There is the matter of
ceremonial dress.

As you know, I am very
cautious about any unprotected
contact with the alien germs
on this highly messy planet.
Keeping my person clear of
Earthling molecules has not
been easy.

But aware as I am of the
constant threat of infestation,
I have made hygiene a top-level
priority.

My best means of protection is of course my Federation uniform, and I do my best to keep it on at all times.

Without my uniform I am
vulnerable to whatever toxicity
is swarming around in their
murky atmosphere. On several
occasions I have been struck
down by mysterious Earthly
diseases.

Mothership:

*Inconceivable that a
Federation officer
should ever be exposed
in such a way!*

Too true. Unfortunately, during festival events, the Maternal and Paternal Units can

be quite insistent that I don
one of their absurd ceremonial
costumes.

I do my best to resist
them. But on this occasion,
resistance was futile.

Mothership:

*And so
you agreed to
attend the festival
without your
protective uniform?*

I had no choice, Mothership.
I must blend in with their
culture if I am to truly study
them in depth.

I took whatever precautions
I could and prepared to face
their atmosphere.

44

Mothership:

*Have you been able
to discern
the reason for
their irrational fear?*

It stems from the beings they
call relatives (genetically
linked mini-brains). And I must
say, Mothership, that they have
reason to be fearful.

Mothership:

*Can you describe
these creatures?*

Amongst the most frightening of the genetically linked MBs are the two I refer to as Alpha Nana and Beta Nana. Alpha Nana is the more aggressive of the two. I believe that she may in fact be a cannibal.

However, Beta Nana is
equally terrifying. She has
attempted to suffocate me on
more than one occasion.
  Neither seems to have any
sense of common decency.

When Alpha Nana and Beta
Nana are united, they create an

energy field that disrupts
everything in its path.

They are often in the company
of The Two-Headed Obnoxatron.
One head is called Nelson
and the other is called Howard,
but I admit that I cannot
always tell which is which.

Perhaps the result of some genetic experiment gone horribly, horribly wrong, The Obnoxatron lumbers about in its brutish way, crushing all those unfortunate enough to cross its path.

53

Conversing with this behemoth is next to impossible as it possesses a vocabulary of only ten or perhaps fifteen words.

UH-HUNH: Affirmative

YEAH!: I find this situation pleasing.

GROSS: I find this object/food/situation unpleasant.

LOSER!: An insult, usually directed at those who do not appreciate their clumsy games

DUFUS!: see LOSER!

DORK.: see DUFUS!

DUH?: A show of sarcasm, expressing disbelief

NUH-UH: Negative

WHATEVER, DUDE: This one is unclear to me. I believe it is a display of superiority or indifference.

Mothership:

*Didn't you do battle
with a similar creature
during your brief
experiment with
the martial arts?*

I think I had that incident erased from my memory bank. In any case, these festivals are excellent opportunities to observe the mini-brains in a different mode.

But my note taking irritates
them and I am often forced to
do it in secret.

Mothership:

Tell us, Rodriguez.
We are intrigued
by your dealings with
The Obnoxatron.
How do you manage
to coexist with this
low-level life-form?

Although we could not be more
different from one another,
our respective Parental Units
insist on seeing all Earthling
juveniles as a unified crew.
The Obnoxatron and I are
ordered about in a group, and
sometimes forced to interact
with an item known as a ball.

Mothership:

A ball?

A type of orb.

Mothership:

An orb?

Yes, Mothership. And this ORB, how it tortures me! It is nothing but a cheap synthetic polymer formed into the shape of a sphere or pointed egg, but the mini-brains worship it as though it had magical powers.

Kick ball	Menacing rubber orb, often aimed at face or rear end
Softball	Allegedly "soft" orb, still capable of causing pain when lobbed at stomach or forehead with wooden club
Basketball	Pockmarked orange polymer orb, favored by the taller Earthlings; must be shoved through unattainable hoop
Golf ball	Tiny white orb, moved about from tiny hole to tiny hole while on long and excruciatingly boring walks

Mothership:

Ah. We see.
It is a
ceremonial
object.

Precisely. There are different orbs for different "games," and the most sacred of all orbs is the pointed egg. This was the object that was to be the focus of our "game."

The mini-brains cannot rest at festival time until the egg has been tossed about for at least an hour.

67

68

Over and over they came at me
with it.

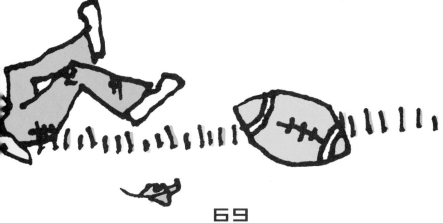

Finally, The Obnoxatron grew
weary of attacking me.

Upon our return to the communal area, I was greeted with expressions of displeasure and disgust as the mini-brains observed my state.

71

I gladly made use of the opportunity to change back into my protective uniform. When I returned to the communal area, I was a shining example of Federation pride. Unfortunately, I neglected to put on a helmet.

Mothership:

A helmet?
As far as we know,
a helmet is not
included in your
standard uniform.

No, Mothership, it is not.
But a helmet might have
shielded me from the
impending attack.

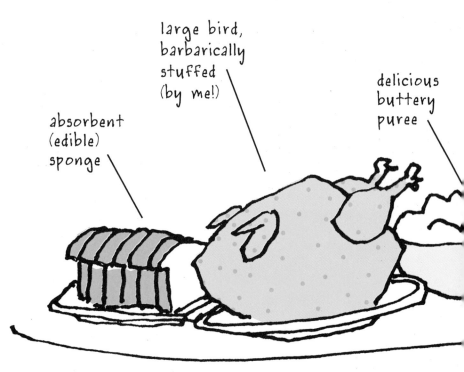

large bird,
barbarically
stuffed
(by me!)

delicious
buttery
puree

absorbent
(edible)
sponge

Allow me to set the scene.
The ceremonial table groans
beneath the weight of a
thousand different dishes.
Many of the foods are brown.

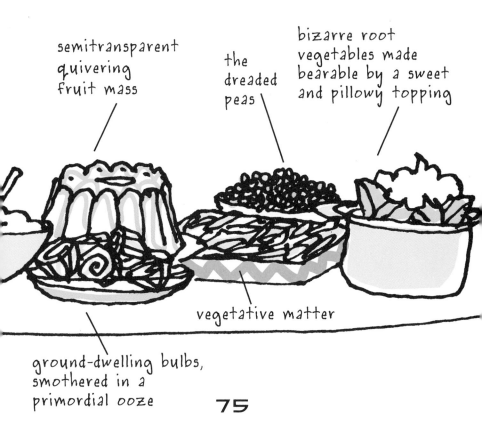

semitransparent
quivering
fruit mass

the
dreaded
peas

bizarre root
vegetables made
bearable by a sweet
and pillowy topping

vegetative matter

ground-dwelling bulbs,
smothered in a
primordial ooze

As an initial offering,
Beta Nana presented us with
a scalding urn brimming with
a dubious substance. She
was obviously proud of this
disgusting concoction, and it
was made clear to me that I
was expected to eat mass
quantities of the swampy mess.

Mothership:

And were you able
to consume
a sufficient amount
of the Earthling food?

Of course, Mothership.
Refusing to partake in their
feast would have deeply
insulted the mini-brains. I
would never want to jeopardize
my position here.

I am first and foremost a scientist, so I did my best to investigate the ingredients that made up the mysterious concoction.

The crafty creature was determined to withhold her secrets.

The flavor was not
unacceptable. As for the
ingredients, I will never know,
Mothership. I will never know.
I have been feeling queasy ever
since. Unfortunately, it's too
late to beam up a sample for
analysis.

86

Mothership:

*Your report both
horrifies and fascinates.
Still, we wish to inquire,
how do these events
relate to your
current state
of infection?*

As the rest of the MBs gave
in to their gluttony, Alpha
Nana seemed distracted. She
zeroed in on me with a strange
look in her eyes.

82

Mothership:

*Was the creature
hypnotized by
your appearance?
The majesty of
your uniform?*

No, Mothership. The creature
was intent on infecting me.

Mothership:

Infecting you?

Yes.

Before I could stop it, it clutched me and rendered me helpless.

Then it licked its claw, reached out, and attempted to

infect me with a glistening gob
of its genetic material!

Mothership:

Horrifying!

Horrifying indeed.

I do not know if I have made you aware of this, Mothership, but the human mouth is a hotbed of disease.

Mothership:

These beings are clearly a very low type of life-form!

The mini-brains believe it is they who rule the Earth, but it is really the germs who control everything.

As quietly as possible,
I excused myself from the
festivities and proceeded to
the sanitization chamber.

The mini-brains reacted as
if my emergency were of no
importance, laughing at me as

though I had been genetically engineered for their amusement.

Mothership:

Were you able
to detoxify
in time?

I believe so, Mothership. It has been some time since the contamination and I have yet to suffer any ill effects. Perhaps I will . . .

WAIT!!!

Mothership:

What is it,
First Officer?

Evilomami approaches. I
hear the clicking of her
dimension-altering footwear
as she marches down the
stairs.

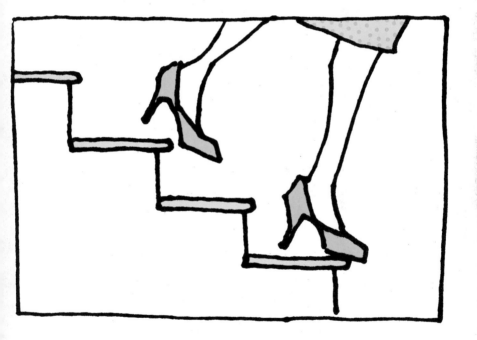

Mothership:

What's going on,
First Officer?

I am under attack! Evilomami
is demanding that I return
to the scene of my potential
infection. Voltron only knows
what they have in store for me.

Mothership:

*We cannot risk
reinfection!
Your entire mission
is in jeopardy!*

Too true. Too true.
Shall we destroy them? This
Germ Warfare goes against
all Federation law!

Perhaps that is the only
option. I do not know if
I could survive another
onslaught.

106

Mothership:

*Prepare for
molecular transmission,
First Officer Rodriguez!
As soon as your
reintegration is complete,
we will blow
the entire planet
to smithereens!*

Wait!
Mothership,
stop
molecular
transmission!

Mothership:

What is it,
First Officer Rodriguez?

There is
something else.
A delicious
aroma.

Not the
usual smell of
Earthling food.
No . . .
something much
more enticing.

Can it be?
Yes . . .
it is!

Mothership:

What?

EMPANADAS!!

Mothership:

Empanadas?

Yes, Mothership! Empanadas!!
Ah, Mothership. As you know,
it will not be a sad day for
me when my mission on this
grubby little blue marble comes
to an end. The beings here
are limited both mentally and
physically, and their primitive
nature has been a trial to me
from the first.

However . . . I must admit,
there are a few aspects of
Earthling culture of which I
have grown fond. I have already
written to you extensively about
the wonder of cartoons, but
I believe I have never really
conveyed to you the glory of the
Earthling food called EMPANADA.

Oh, the name is like music
to me, Mothership. EMPANADA!
EMPANADA! EMPANADA! The only
thing more pleasing than
talking about them is eating
them.

Mothership:

We are not sure
we understand.

They are like small pockets
of joy. I find them almost
irresistible.

A crisp yet tender
envelope of dough,
which contains a
delightfully savory
filling.

Perhaps I should remain on
Earth a while longer while I
determine whether or not the
planet should be destroyed.

Mothership:

First Officer!
Control yourself!
Think of your safety!

An officer of the Federation cannot allow himself to be swayed by a few whiffs of an Earthling delicacy!

Of course, Mothership. But perhaps the empanada itself is proof that the mini-brains should be given another chance. Beings that can create something this perfect must have some redeeming qualities.

I feel it is my duty to remain here and study their complexities in depth.

Mothership:

Then you will . . .

Yes, Mothership. I will
return to the communal table
and rejoin the mini-brains in
their primitive revelries.

124

Mothership:

*But what
of the risks
to your
personal safety?*

You and I both know that RISK is my middle name. And now I must sign off. Duty calls!

Mothership:

Very well.
All hail
the Federation!

130

Published by Scholastic Press, an imprint of Scholastic Inc.,
Publishers since 1920. SCHOLASTIC, SCHOLASTIC PRESS, and
associated logos are trademarks and/or registered trademarks
of Scholastic Inc.

LIBRARY OF CONGRESS CATALOGING-IN-PUBLICATION DATA

Stadler, Alexander.
Invasion of the Relatives / Alexander Stadler. —1st ed.
p. cm. —(Julian Rodriguez ; episode 2)
Summary: First Officer Julian Rodriguez, imaginary space warrior,
must endure the odious and unhygienic festivities of genetically
linked mini-brains when members of his extended family visit over
the holidays.
ISBN-13: 978-0-439-91967-8
ISBN-10: 0-439-91967-3
[1. Imagination —Fiction. 2. Extraterrestrial beings —Fiction.
3. Family —Fiction. 4. Humorous stories.]
I. Title. PZ7.S7754In 2009   [Fic] —dc22   2008039528

10 9 8 7 6 5 4 3 2 1   09 10 11 12 13

Printed in the U.S.A.   23
First edition, September 2009

WE TRY TO PRODUCE THE MOST BEAUTIFUL BOOKS POSSIBLE AND WE ARE
EXTREMELY CONCERNED ABOUT THE IMPACT OF OUR MANUFACTURING PROCESS
ON THE FORESTS OF THE WORLD AND THE ENVIRONMENT AS A WHOLE.
ACCORDINGLY, WE MADE SURE THAT THE PAPER USED IN THIS BOOK HAS BEEN
CERTIFIED AS COMING FROM FORESTS THAT ARE MANAGED TO INSURE THE
PROTECTION OF THE PEOPLE AND WILDLIFE DEPENDENT UPON THEM.

This book was mostly written at The Beauty Shop Café
at the corner of 20th and Fitzwater Street.
Intergalactic thank-yous to Christine Chisolm;
Chris Bartlett; Claire Shubik; Maryann Connolly; my
parents, John and Charlotte Stadler; Darrin Britting;
Sarah Stadler; Elizabeth Dow and Linda Sylvester;
Lori McLean; Donna Paul; Antonio DaMotta;
Sarah Maceneany; Jane Brodie and Simon B.;
Dr. Ruth Greenberg; The Eisenberg Solloway Family;
Josephine Albarelli; Jamie Bishton; Elena Sisto;
Marcy Hermansader; Catherine Coquillard; Joy Bouldin;
Fergie Cary and Wee Eamon; Ernie Sesskin and
Brian Foster; technical wizardess Claire Iltis;
Debbie Hochman Turvey; The Mazza Museum in Findlay,
Ohio; The Rosenbach Museum and Library in
Philadelphia; my siblings Jenny Stadler,
Iyana Stadler, Eliot Stadler, Daniel Stadler, and
David Stadler; Barbara Carter; Carolyn Carter;
and last but never in a million light-years least,
Julian Carter.

This book was edited by Kara LaReau. The interior pages were art directed, designed, and typeset by Marijka Kostiw. The interior art was created using pen and ink on paper and was digitally colored by Alexander Stadler. The cover was designed by Steve Scott.

The text was set in OCR-A, a font created in 1968 by the American Type Founders. The interior type for the Mothership was set in Break, a GarageFont. The voice bubble and label type were set in Schmalex2000, a font custom created from Alex Stadler's own hand lettering.

Production of this book was supervised by Joy Simpkins, and manufacturing was supervised by Jess White. The book was printed and bound at R. R. Donnelly.

DON'T MISS
FIRST OFFICER JULIAN RODRIGUEZ
IN EPISODE ONE:
Trash Crisis on Earth!

First he's denied his midday nutrition
capsule (lunch). Then he's faced with a day of
standardized testing at his education center
(school) and an ambush by girl-bullies.
But the greatest humiliation comes when Julian
must face his archenemy (who just happens to
bear an uncanny resemblance to his mother).

CAN OUR HERO PREVAIL?